Word List

Here is a list of words that might make it easier to read this book. You'll find them in boldface the first time they appear in the story.

excited	ek-SYT-id
generations	jen-uh-RAY-shuns
buried	BER-eed
quilt	kwilt
embroidered	em-BROI-derd
design	di-ZINE
seamstress	SEEM-stris
traditional	truh-DISH-uhn-ul
doubloon	dub-LOON
portrait	POR-trit
heirlooms	AIR-looms
historians	his-TOR-ee-uhns

Barbie™

A Stitch in Time

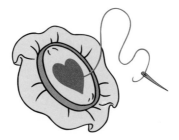

Grolier Books

Barbie took a deep breath of salty ocean air. She was sitting next to the captain of a small boat. He was steering them to an island off the coast of South Carolina. Everywhere Barbie looked, the clear blue sky met the deep blue sea.

"Do we have much farther to go?" she asked the captain.

The white-haired man nodded his head. "You can't see the island until we're almost there. But we're getting closer to it now."

Barbie took off her sunglasses. Sure enough, she could see the tiny shape of the island begin to appear.

Barbie was on her way to visit her friend Mary, who lived on the coastal island. Barbie had not seen her in a long time. Mary's letters were filled with stories about the island. She wrote about her friendly neighbors. She also wrote about her family's farm on the island. Barbie had always wanted to see Mary's home. Now that she was almost there, Barbie was very **excited** about seeing her friend again.

The boat slowed down as a wooden dock came into view. The captain tied up the boat. Barbie could see Mary waving to her from the shore.

"Watch your step," said the captain. He placed Barbie's bags onto the dock. Barbie thanked him. Then she greeted Mary with a warm hug.

"You made it!" Mary cried happily. "How was your trip?"

"Wonderful!" said Barbie. Mary and Barbie left the dock. As they walked to Mary's car, Barbie looked around. Old wooden houses lined the street. The windows of each house had boxes filled with bright flowers. "It's so pretty here," Barbie said.

Mary agreed. "I really love this island."

Barbie put her bags into the trunk of Mary's old car.

"The farm has been in my family for almost two hundred years," Mary explained as she drove. "My sisters, cousins, and I always spent our summers there when we were children. Then, not long ago, it seemed that my family would have to sell the farm. No one was using it any longer. So I decided to come live here on the island. It's the best move I've ever made!"

Barbie looked out the car window. She could see why Mary loved the island. Barbie saw children splashing in a sparkling stream. Goats grazed in a green meadow nearby. People smiled and waved at Mary's car as she drove past them.

"I love it already," Barbie said. "Everyone seems so friendly."

"This is a small town," said Mary. "People get to know each other pretty well." Soon she turned the car down a dusty road.

Chapter Two

"Here we are!" Mary declared. They pulled up to an old farmhouse with white shutters. Hens and chicks scattered as the two friends walked up the path.

"Watch your head!" Mary said as they entered. "The doorways are very low. That's the way they built houses a long time ago."

Barbie bent down a little and stepped into the kitchen. Old wooden floors creaked under her feet. In front of her was a huge fireplace.

"This is the oldest part of the house," Mary explained. "The kitchen was where families of long ago spent most of their time. It was always built first. The other rooms were added on later when they were needed."

"I really love old furniture," Mary went on. "I guess you could say I collect it. This old cradle has been in my family for **generations**."

Barbie admired the sturdy wooden cradle. "It's beautiful. And it looks so at home here."

Mary nodded. "Modern things would look out of place in an old house like this," she said and smiled. "But have no fear, I do at least have a television set."

Barbie laughed as Mary gave her a tour of the other rooms.

Finally Mary showed Barbie to the guest bedroom.

"Why don't you get unpacked," Mary suggested. "I'll show you the rest of the farm when you're ready."

"Sounds great!" Barbie replied.

Barbie quickly put her clothes away. Then she went downstairs to join Mary outside.

Barbie and Mary walked down a hill to a small cove. They stood on the beach and watched families enjoying the ocean.

"This island is a popular vacation spot now," Mary told Barbie. "But when my family first came here, pirate ships were still sailing into this very cove. There are legends of treasure being **buried** here. But no one has ever found anything. Still, the tales of pirates and treasure help to bring the tourists here every summer."

"Do you think treasure might be buried on your farm?" Barbie asked.

Mary laughed. "When we were kids, we used to dig for pirate treasure. But we never found one bit of gold! Grandma used to tell us a family riddle about buried treasure. Let me see if I can remember it now."

Mary thought for a moment. "It's been such

a long time." Her face suddenly brightened. "Oh, yes, I do remember it after all."

"Please," said Barbie, "I'd love to hear it."

Mary smiled and said:

If love's treasure you wish to find,
Take thirty steps and a stitch in time!

"What does it mean?" asked Barbie.

Mary giggled. "Grandma would send us to hunt treasure whenever she wanted to get work done. We would spend hours trying to solve the riddle. None of us could ever figure it out."

Barbie started to think about the riddle. But Mary wanted to show her more of the farm.

"Come on," said Mary, leading Barbie toward the barn. "I have a little friend that I'd like you to meet!"

Barbie spent the rest of the afternoon visiting the animals who lived on the farm. First they

petted the woolly lamb and its mother. Then it was time to milk the cow and pick vegetables. After all that work, Barbie and Mary were very hot. They decided to go wading in the brook. By dinnertime, the two friends were starving, so they headed back to the house.

"A long day on the farm really makes people hungry," Mary said when dinner was ready. She piled Barbie's plate with the vegetables they had picked.

Barbie could hardly believe that earlier in the day she had been in a busy city. At this moment, the only sound she heard was ocean waves.

"Thank you for dinner," said Barbie. "Now tell me more about this island of yours."

"There's so much to tell," Mary said, "I don't know where to begin. That's why I think an island museum is so important."

"Do you think we could go there tomorrow?" Barbie asked.

Mary shook her head. "It's not even built yet," she sighed. "I'm helping to raise money for the museum. We have an old house to use for it. But we still have a long way to go. I'm hoping my newest idea will help."

With that, Mary stood up and opened an old trunk in the corner. "What do you think?" she asked. She held up an unfinished **quilt**. The quilt was made of different squares of cloth sewn together. More stitches were **embroidered** across the whole piece. This gave the quilt a bumpy, wrinkled look. There was a fabric square of a boat and one of a heart.

"Did you make this yourself?" Barbie asked.

Mary nodded. "I'm going to sell it when it's finished and give the money to the museum," she said proudly. "But quilting takes a long time."

Barbie took the cloth in her hands for a better look. "It looks like a jigsaw puzzle made of cloth! Can I make a square?" Barbie asked. "I can't sew as well as you can. But if you show me how I'd love to try and help."

"Barbie, that's a wonderful idea!" Mary cried. "I would love to have someone quilt with me. Years ago, that's how a lot of quilts were made. Groups of women got together and sewed. Visiting and talking with one another made the time go by a lot faster."

"That sounds like fun!" Barbie replied. She studied Mary's squares more closely. "What kind of **design** should my square be?" she wondered.

"Well, it should have something to do with the island," Mary suggested. "I know. Tomorrow we'll go into town. There are lots of interesting things to see. Maybe you'll get an idea there."

"Great!" answered Barbie. "I can't wait!"

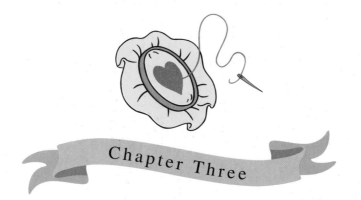

Chapter Three

The next morning, Barbie woke up to the smell of freshly baked bread. She hopped out of bed and opened the window. A breeze blew back her hair as she breathed in the fresh air.

"This is one of the most beautiful places I've ever seen!" she exclaimed. She quickly dressed in jeans and a pink shirt and went downstairs.

In the kitchen, Mary was already busily stitching away. She put down her sewing when Barbie entered the room.

"Barbie, you've got me excited about this island all over again," she told her friend. "I'm so happy that you're going to help me with the quilt. You have given me an idea for another square. It's a picture of the apple orchard at harvest time."

Barbie grinned. "That's a great idea," she said. "I had better get started on my square!"

Barbie asked for some paper. As she ate her breakfast, she drew ideas for her square. But she quickly crumpled up each picture.

"Maybe I should leave the quilting to you," Barbie said, laughing.

Mary laughed, too. "Nonsense," Mary said. "I'm sure you'll come up with a wonderful design."

"I'll keep trying!" said Barbie.

"Here, let me show you something that may help," Mary said. She left the room and returned carrying an old quilt wrapped in tissue paper.

"This quilt has been in my family for generations," she told Barbie.

Mary gently unfolded the quilt. It was beautiful, even with some faded and stained parts. Mary and Barbie cleared the breakfast dishes from the table. Then they carefully spread the quilt out over the kitchen table.

Barbie looked at the quilt. "I love it," she said.

"Thank you," answered Mary. "I love it, too. I never get tired of looking at it. The quilting over the fabric is amazing. Someone long ago was a skilled **seamstress**! I hope to put this in a special place in the museum someday. It's my favorite thing in the world. But I want other people to enjoy it, too."

Barbie looked at the quilt more carefully. She saw that the whole thing had been sewn by hand. Mary was right. It *did* belong in a museum.

"Wow!" said Barbie. "This is a real work of art. Since the museum isn't open yet, why don't you hang this up in your house. It would look perfect in your living room!"

"It would be nice to look at it all the time. But I don't want anything to happen to it," Mary said. She smiled. "I don't take it out that often. But I'm happy to show it off to special guests."

"Thank you for sharing it with me," said Barbie. "I feel lucky to be seeing it!"

"Some things about this quilt have always puzzled me, though," Mary said. She pointed at some of the stitching. "I've never understood why this stitching seems to have been done in an odd pattern. Also, most of the sewing is very well done. But then there is this part." She pointed to an area of uneven stitching. "I wonder if a little girl practiced on this square."

Barbie looked closely at the uneven stitches. They puzzled her, too. Then she suddenly asked, "Mary, do you have a hand mirror?"

"Sure," answered Mary. "Why?"

"I have a hunch about this stitching," Barbie said thoughtfully.

Mary got a hand mirror and gave it to her friend. Barbie held the mirror next to the stitching. "I was right!" she cried. "Look, Mary! It's a name."

Sure enough, the tiny stitches spelled a name. The quilter had stitched the letters backwards. The name could only be read in a mirror.

"Marietta," Mary read out loud.

"Was she the woman who made the quilt?" Barbie asked.

"Maybe," Mary said. "But I never heard that name in my family before."

Suddenly Mary jumped up and ran to a closet. "Let's look in my old family album," she said. "Years ago, families used to write the births, marriages, and deaths inside the cover. Perhaps we'll find a clue there!"

"Okay," said Barbie when Mary had brought the book. "Let's see what we've got." Her eyes searched the pages.

But nowhere did the old album mention the

name *Marietta*. "Too bad," said Mary. "I guess we'll never know who Marietta was."

"Don't give up so soon!" Barbie told her friend. If there was anything Barbie loved, it was a mystery. And this was beginning to look like an interesting one!

Chapter Four

The friends decided to go off to the town hall to search for clues. They wanted to check Mary's family records there for the name *Marietta*. Mary and Barbie made the short drive to town. Soon they walked up to the town hall's big wooden information desk.

Barbie and Mary explained to the man behind the desk what they were looking for and why.

"How interesting!" the man exclaimed. "I was helping one young man search through his family records. We found an old photo of a pirate that looked just like the young man. The pirate was his long-lost uncle! I wish you luck! The records you are looking for are right this way," he said, leading them to a row of dusty old books.

Barbie and Mary thanked him. They began to search the many yellowed pages of the town's history books.

The friends looked through wills, marriage certificates, and photographs. But there was no record anywhere of a woman named Marietta.

"Achoo!" Mary sneezed, as she held up a dusty old newspaper.

"Achoo!" Barbie sneezed in response. The friends burst out laughing. "Maybe it's time for some lunch and fresh air?" Barbie asked. She wiped the dust from her hands.

"I couldn't agree more!" Mary replied.

After they had eaten, the friends walked in the bright afternoon sunshine. "Come on," Mary said. "Let's go to the fabric shop and see if we can get some cloth for your quilt square."

"I'm still not sure what I'm going to put on it," Barbie replied, "but choosing the fabric might give me some ideas."

Tiny bells jingled on the shop door as Barbie and Mary stepped inside. Fabrics of all colors and patterns were stacked floor to ceiling.

"May I help you?" asked the shopkeeper. She put the embroidery she was working on behind the counter.

Barbie shook her head in wonder at all the different fabrics. "I don't even know where to begin!" she said with a laugh. Quickly she explained to the woman about Mary's project. Then Barbie told her about the quilt square she wanted to make. Mary finished by telling the shopkeeper about the mysterious name stitched into her family quilt.

The woman's eyes sparkled as she listened. "Oh, I love a good mystery!" she exclaimed. "And this island is full of them! Come with me!"

The elderly woman led Barbie and Mary down an aisle crowded with fabric, ribbons, and rainbow-colored threads.

She reached into a drawer and pulled out a heavy book. "This book shows many of the **traditional** patterns used for quilting," she said. "Perhaps you may recognize the pattern of the old quilt in here. And even if you don't, you may get an idea for your new quilt."

Barbie took the book and began to flip through the pages.

"Each of the patterns in the book has a meaning," said the woman. "Quilting was often the best way for women to be creative. Each quilt was a very special thing to make. Quilts often told stories, too. See, there are patterns for births and deaths, marriages and harvests, and even dreams."

"How about pirates?" Mary asked.

"Perhaps," the woman replied. "But if I

were to tell a story about pirates, I would not just stitch a picture of a pirate ship. That would be too obvious. You need to look more closely at your family's old quilt. There may be more to it than meets the eye."

"The quilt has an odd design," Barbie said. "We think maybe two different people worked on it. Some of the stitches are so perfect and even and follow a pattern. But if you look closer, you can see stitches and lines going off in zigzags and curves, with no pattern at all. It just doesn't make sense."

"They still may have been sewn by the same hand. Many experienced quilters began their quilts by making some sort of mistake on purpose. This way, they reminded themselves that no one is perfect," the shopkeeper laughed.

The woman opened a drawer and handed Barbie a stack of tracing paper. "I have a suggestion," she said. "It may be easier to understand the message in your quilt if you are not looking at all the different colors and pieces of fabric. Just trace the stitching. Copy what you see, and you may find your answer."

Barbie and Mary thought this was a wonderful idea.

"Just make sure to be extra careful," the woman warned. "Trace lightly so you don't write on the quilt underneath."

"Of course," Barbie said. "I understand." Thanking the woman, she and Mary left the shop.

As Mary's car bumped along the narrow road, Barbie began to laugh.

"What's so funny?" Mary asked.

"I was so interested in finding out about the old quilt, I forgot all about buying fabric for the new one!" she exclaimed as they drove away from town.

Mary laughed. "You're right!" she said.

"But let's not turn back now. I can't wait to

get home to take another peek at that quilt," said
Barbie.

"Me either!" Mary said. "We're almost there.
On this island you can get anywhere you need to
go in the blink of an eye!"

Chapter Five

Back at the house, Barbie and Mary spread out the old quilt on the table once again.

"Shoo!" Mary said as her cat leapt on top.

Barbie reached over to brush aside some stray cat hairs and stopped suddenly. "Mary, look at this," she said.

Barbie's finger followed the design on the blue border. It went up and down, up and down. "Let's start by tracing the stitching on the border pattern. I have a hunch about it!" She grabbed a pencil and carefully began to draw on the tracing paper.

"Aha!" Barbie shouted as she held up her

drawing. "Just as I thought!"

Mary frowned. "I don't get it," she admitted.

"These are waves! Ocean waves! See? The blue fabric was used here on purpose. The border is meant to be the ocean!" Barbie exclaimed.

"Barbie! You're right!" Mary cried.

The two friends each took a corner of the quilt to trace onto the paper. "Now let's see what else we can find," said Barbie.

The friends studied the tracing. The neat pattern of waves turned into jagged lines with no familiar shape. After a while, Mary put down her pencil. "I'm not coming up with anything," she said with a yawn.

"I'm not either," Barbie sighed. "I really thought we were onto something."

"I'd hoped we'd find more names, or dates, or even an outline of something," Mary said.

"Why would someone go to all the trouble of making the border look like the ocean?" Barbie said. "The middle part of the quilt seems to be stitched any old way."

"Don't people often name ships after women?" Mary said. "Maybe Marietta is not a person at all."

"Mary, you're a genius!" Barbie said. "Maybe we're tracing a picture of a pirate ship in the middle of the ocean! Let's keep going and see what it looks like."

The two friends continued tracing, but the shape they ended up with was quite an odd-looking one.

"This is so strange!" Mary said. "No pirate would last on a ship shaped like this!"

Barbie giggled. "If I were Marietta, and someone named this after me, I think I'd be very insulted!" She thought for a moment. "Maybe it's not meant to be a pirate ship, but something else."

"But what?" Mary wondered aloud.

"It's just one more mystery to solve!" said Barbie.

"Then let's look for clues at the beach," Mary said. "I think we deserve a break."

"So do I!" agreed Barbie. So the two friends gathered some towels and books and spent the rest of the day at the shore.

Chapter Six

Later that evening, Barbie went up to the guest bedroom and changed into her pajamas.

"Marietta. Marietta," she repeated as she stared at the tracing. "I wonder if this was her room. I wonder if she was in love with a pirate. Did she watch the ships from this very window?" Barbie daydreamed.

"I've got to stop thinking about this," she decided. "Sometimes it's easier to solve things if you just forget about them for a while." She put the drawing aside and looked through her bag for a pen and some postage stamps. Then she lay down on the bed and began to write postcards.

Dear Ken,
It's been a wonderful trip so far. I know you would
love the beautiful beaches here. As you can see
from this postcard, this island was the perfect
place for . . .

Barbie sat up suddenly and flipped the postcard over. A map of the island was on the front.

"Mary!" Barbie shouted. She jumped off the bed and went to find her friend.

Barbie showed Mary the postcard and the tracing from the quilt. The map on the postcard matched their tracing almost perfectly.

"Amazing," said Mary. "Whoever Marietta was, she sure didn't miss a thing. She stitched a map of the whole island on the quilt!" Mary exclaimed.

Then Mary looked more closely at the tracing. "Look," she said, pointing, "here's where the town is, here's the cove, and here's my farm."

Barbie lifted up the tracing to look at the quilt. "And look! Your farm has the same stitching as the island outline. And there's even more unusual stitching here!"

"You're right!" Mary said. She was excited at this new discovery.

The friends got pencils and started to trace the area where Mary's farm appeared. Soon they began to see dots, dashes, and squiggles.

They stared at the tracing. It took them a few minutes before they realized that Mary's house, barn, and drinking well were all there. They even saw a tiny X placed halfway between the house and the well.

"I think this is a treasure map!" Barbie exclaimed.

"And X marks the spot!" the friends said at

the same time.

Mary jumped up. "Do you think there's really buried treasure here on the farm?" she asked.

Barbie grew serious for a moment. "Well, an X could mean anything," she began.

Then she gave Mary a playful grin. "But if this is a treasure map, then the X can only mean one thing. And you think so, too!"

Mary smiled. "It would be wonderful if you are right," she answered. "But what if nothing is there? This quilt was made such a long time ago. Maybe we're not the first ones to figure out its secret."

"Well, there's only one way to find out," Barbie said. "Buried treasure, here we come!"

Mary and Barbie put on their shoes, grabbed a couple of flashlights, and headed outside.

"Now what do we do?" asked Mary. "This yard is huge. How do we know where to start digging?"

"Hey, wait a minute," Barbie said, snapping

her fingers. "What was that family riddle your grandmother used to tell you?"

Mary slowly repeated the riddle:

If love's treasure you wish to find,
Take thirty steps and a stitch in time!

The friends looked at each other and dashed back to the front door of Mary's house. Slowly, they counted thirty steps toward the drinking well. They came to a stop halfway between the house and the well.

"This is it," Barbie said. The two friends shone their flashlights down at the grass.

"I've crossed this spot a hundred times," Mary said. "I was going to start a garden here in the next couple of weeks. I never dreamed this place was so important."

"I guess it's true that to find adventure you don't need to look any further than your own backyard," Barbie laughed.

Mary smiled. "But what should we do now?" she asked. "It's too dark to really do any digging."

Barbie agreed. "Besides, this may take a lot of shoveling," she said. "Who knows how deep the treasure is buried. Do you know anyone who could help us tomorrow?"

"Of course!" Mary declared. "Everyone on the island will be interested in this," she laughed. "It's the kind of adventure islanders live for!"

And so back to the house they went. Once inside, Mary made some phone calls and invited her friends over at eight o'clock the next morning for a big breakfast before the dig. Getting into the spirit, Barbie found some red fabric and loosely stitched a big X to put outside.

That night, each of them drifted off to sleep wondering what kind of surprises the next day's dig might bring.

Chapter Seven

The next morning, both Barbie and Mary woke up extra early. By seven forty-five, cars began to drive up Mary's driveway. Mary and Barbie rushed out to greet everyone. The visitors had brought shovels and some rope.

"Yo-ho-ho!" called out a young man wearing an eye patch. He flipped up the patch and winked at Mary. "Just thought I'd get in the spirit of things." Then he turned to Barbie and introduced himself. "Hi! My name is John. But you can call me 'Cap'n' for today."

Barbie laughed and introduced herself. Soon

tugged on the rope he had tied. Their feet slipped in the dirt, but soon the heavy trunk was pulled out.

The group was quiet as Mary knelt to brush the dirt off the trunk.

"Look!" she cried. "There are initials engraved in the top! And the date 1796!"

Everyone gasped. "Open it up!" said John. "We can't wait another minute!"

Mary gave the old lock a tug, and the rusty metal broke in two. She lifted the trunk's lid carefully. The rusty metal hinges creaked and groaned.

Mary's friends gathered around the trunk and held their breath. Was there really treasure inside? Suddenly they had their answer.

"Candlesticks!" Mary cried. "And a vase! And look at these old spoons!" Then she found a small framed painting of a serious-looking man and woman.

"That looks like a wedding **portrait**,"

John said.

"A wedding portrait?" Mary said in disbelief. "They don't look very happy. And the bride isn't even wearing a veil!"

The older man spoke up again. "A lot has changed over the years," he explained. "Having a portrait painted was a serious business. It meant posing for a long time, paying an artist, and dressing up in your best clothes. Farmers didn't usually spend money on luxuries such as this. But I guess this couple thought it was worth it. This painting might be more valuable today than all the things in that trunk combined!"

"But why would someone bury their belongings in the yard?" Barbie asked.

"I think I can explain that," said John. "Pirates often came to the island. People who lived here took care to hide their things from them. These objects must have been very important to your relatives, Mary. Maybe they hoped to save them for future members of their family, like you."

Barbie reached into the chest. "I think these might have been wedding gifts," she said. She gently placed two narrow bands of gold in Mary's hand. They were tied together with a silk ribbon. "Here are the wedding rings."

Mary read what was engraved inside the rings: MT and JT, 1796. "Is *M* for *Marietta?*" she wondered. She hoped she would have her answer soon.

Everyone settled down to a picnic lunch to rest and discuss what they had found. Barbie read the notes she had made at the town hall out loud. "I have a Mary and a Jacob marrying that year, but not a Marietta," she told them.

John explained, "Whoever recorded the marriage probably could not read or spell that well. A lot of farmers did not have the chance for an education back then. Maybe because *Mary* was a lot easier to write, that's what was recorded. I'll bet *Mary* was a nickname for *Marietta.*"

"So that's how my name became a family name," Mary said.

"Since 1796," John said with a smile.

"You know, Mary," said Barbie, "we may not have uncovered gold doubloons, but this is a truly valuable treasure."

"I know," Mary replied. "What is in that trunk is a piece of my family's history."

"What are you going to do with these things?" John asked Mary.

"They belong in the museum we're planning, of course," she replied. "Why do you ask?"

"Well, I know these are family **heirlooms**," John began, "but some **historians** would pay you a lot of money to buy them. Then you would have the money for your museum."

Barbie leaned on her shovel and smiled. "Seems like this new treasure sure has given you a lot to think about, Mary," she said.

"I'll say!" said Mary.

Barbie could not believe what a great day it had been. Not only had they discovered buried treasure, but at last she had an idea for her quilt square!

The next day, Barbie packed to go home. "Wow, I can't believe what we found," she said to Mary. "This was the most exciting vacation ever. I can't wait to tell my sisters!"

"I couldn't have done it without you," said Mary. "Promise me you'll come back to visit soon."

Barbie leaned over and gave Mary a hug. "You bet!" she said.

Chapter Eight

Six months later, Barbie returned to the island for another visit. She was sure this visit would be quieter than her last. After all, what could be more exciting than buried treasure?

As the boat docked, John and Mary waved.

"I'm so happy to see you!" Barbie said. "Tell me everything I've missed. No, wait, take me to the museum before we do anything else!"

Mary and John proudly took Barbie to the museum. They explained to Barbie that they had fixed up an old house for the museum, as planned. As she stepped inside the entrance,

Barbie immediately saw the old quilt. It was hanging on a wall under a piece of glass for all to see.

"Oh, Mary!" Barbie said. "You've done a wonderful job with the museum!"

Mary smiled. "It's a dream come true," she said. Then she gave Barbie a tour. "Now everyone who visits the island will have a place to come and learn more about its history. Not only that, they can appreciate some of the beautiful crafts of the people who live here."

"Everything looks fantastic!" Barbie said, looking around.

"Thank you," Mary replied. "But there's more. Remember the historians John talked about who would want to buy some of the things from the trunk?"

"Yes," Barbie replied.

"Well, one of them was touched by my family's story. She let us keep the things for the museum and donated money instead!" said Mary.

"That's great!" Barbie said happily. "But who bought our quilt, Mary?"

John and Mary exchanged glances. Then Mary led Barbie to her tiny office in the museum.

"I never sold it," Mary explained. "Finding the treasure chest helped bring attention to the need for a museum. With so much interest in the island's history, a lot of people donated money. We were so busy, weren't we, John?"

John nodded and gave Mary a smile.

"How exciting!" Barbie exclaimed.

"And it gets better," Mary said, taking John's hand. "Those wedding bands we found are going to be put to good use very soon. We won't even have to change the initials!"

For a second Barbie was confused. Then she realized her friends were getting married!

"Oh, congratulations! Congratulations!" Barbie cried. "Now I know why you haven't had time to write much. Or to finish the quilt."

"Oh, no, it's done," Mary said quickly. She went over to a closet. "I can't thank you enough for uncovering my family's history. But I'd like to try by giving you this." Mary and John unfolded a quilt.

Barbie opened the gift and gasped. "It's the quilt you made!" she cried.

"And it even has your square showing the treasure chest!" Mary pointed out.

"Thank you so much!" said Barbie.

"No, thank *you!*" replied Mary and John at the same time.

"It was my pleasure. I love a good mystery!" Barbie replied. "And who knows, two hundred years from now, someone may find the quilt we made and want to learn more about *us!*"